Sleepless Beauty

Sleepless Beauty

by Frances Minters
illustrated by G. Brian Karas

Viking

J/3K

To Karen and Lew
—F. M.

To MJ and the Wonderful El Oeste
—G. B. K.

The art was prepared with gouache, acrylic, and pencil.

VIKING
Published by the Penguin Group
Penguin Books USA Inc., 375 Hudson Street, New York, New York 10014, U.S.A.
Penguin Books Ltd, 27 Wrights Lane, London W8 5TZ, England
Penguin Books Australia Ltd, Ringwood, Victoria, Australia
Penguin Books Canada Ltd, 10 Alcorn Avenue, Toronto, Ontario, Canada M4V 3B2
Penguin Books (N.Z.) Ltd, 182—190 Wairau Road, Auckland 10, New Zealand

Penguin Books Ltd, Registered Offices: Harmondsworth, Middlesex, England

First published in 1996 by Viking, a division of Penguin Books USA Inc.

1 3 5 7 9 10 8 6 4 2

LIBRARY OF CONGRESS CATALOGING-IN-PUBLICATION DATA
Minters, Frances.
Sleepless Beauty / by Frances Minters.   p. cm.
Summary: In this updated, rhyming retelling of the traditional fairy tale,
Beauty outwits the wicked witch and arranges for her own happy ending.
ISBN 0-670-87033-1
[1. Fairy tales. 2. Folklore. 3. Stories in rhyme.] I. Title.
PZ8.3.M655S1 1996 398.2—dc20 [E] 96-2270 CIP AC

Manufactured in China
Set in OptiArtcraft

Rooty-toot-toot
Rooty-root-tooty,
Here comes the story
of the sleepless beauty.

3/97 B+T

The day I was born
I was such a cutie
Mom and Dad called me
Their own Little Beauty.

They actually named her
Their Little Beauty.

My parents were so happy
To welcome baby me,
They planned a birthday party in
Apartment suite 3D.

They made sure that the cheery news
Was spread throughout the town.
"Just take a bus or subway,
And you're welcome to come down."

All our friends and relatives
Came to the celebration.
But the witch from down the block
Did not receive an invitation.

The witch was just too wicked
to rate an invitation.

The evening of the party
She showed up nonetheless.
Rats and mice played hopscotch
In the pockets of her dress.

The guests crowded our apartment.
The witch didn't seem to mind them.
She simply pushed through to the front,
Though she started way behind them.

She came over to my cradle
And she gave me a big kiss.
She said, "Here is my present
For the pretty little miss."

The witch said, "Now you listen up,
For here's the gift I bring her:
On her fourteenth happy birthday
Little Beauty'll prick her finger.

"Then Beauty and her parents
And everyone who's near
Will fall asleep and stay asleep
For a whole hundred years."

WOW! WHO WOULD WANT TO STAY ASLEEP
FOR A HUNDRED YEARS?

The guests yelled, "You are evil,
And it really isn't fair."
"Okay then," said the wicked witch,
"I'll show you that I care.

"Just to prove I'm not so mean
And that I'm not so snooty,
When time is up, a great rock star
Will wake the Sleeping Beauty."

Booty-toot-toot
And tutti-frutti,
How does that grab you,
Dear little Beauty?

I didn't understand at first,
For I was just a child,
But the witch's scary present
Nearly drove my parents wild.

They thought about it for a while,
And this is what they planned:
Sharp things wouldn't be allowed
To touch my little hand.

They threw out all the knives and forks,
The scissors, every pin,
And everything that they could think
Might prick my tender skin.

Mom and Dad thought Beauty
Had the softest little skin.

As I grew up I noticed,
Though they wouldn't tell me why,
That I couldn't sew on buttons
Or slice an apple pie.

I couldn't cut collages,
I couldn't skate on ice,
I couldn't use a pencil
Till someone used it twice.

I couldn't get a manicure,
I couldn't cut my hair.
Father couldn't shave his face,
But still he didn't care.

He didn't care at all because
he knew what was at stake.
Her mom and dad tried everything
to keep themselves awake.

Then on my fourteenth birthday
My heart went *boom, boom, boom.*
I saw a creepy woman;
She was sitting in my room.

I admit that I was scared
That she might be the witch.
I had made a little plan
But there could be a hitch.

"Well, who are you?" I asked her.
"What are you doing here?"
"I'm delivering your present.
And this is it, my dear."

And then she showed me something
That was black and flat and round.
"It's an old-time vinyl record;
Let's listen to the sound.

"Take hold of the needle
On that doodad over there
And put it on the record—
That's if you're not too scared."

DON'T DO IT BEAUTY!

Well, yes, I touched the needle,
And then I shouted, "Ouch!
I've hurt my little finger!"
So I sat down on the couch.

"Ah ha!" cackled the wicked witch.
"I see I've done my duty.
Good night now for a hundred years.
Sleep well, my Sleeping Beauty."

She vanished in a cloud of smoke
And I yawned very deeply.
I had to take a little nap—
Suddenly, I was sleepy.

Mom and Dad were snoring loud,
So were the dog and cat.
Even a tiny little mouse
Was sleeping on the mat.

Although they couldn't hear me,
"Good night to you," I said.
I put on my pajamas,
And then I went to bed.

see you in a hundred years—
sweet dreams, little beauty.

Next morning bright and early
As always, I awoke.
I saw my parents sleeping—
I thought it was a joke.

"Wake up, wake up!" I shouted.
"You've slept enough, I'd say."
"What year is it?" asked Mother.
"Same year as yesterday."

"We didn't sleep a hundred years?
The witch did us no harm?"
"She couldn't," I said proudly,
" 'Cause I set the alarm."

Yes, folks, I was awakened
By the tuneful sound of rock
Sung by my favorite rock star
On my personal radio clock.

Tickery-tick!
rockity-rock!
Three cheers for little beauty
and her trusty radio clock!

Then Mom and Dad went off to work,
But before I went to school
I sat right down to write a note
To the rock star. It was cool.

MY PLEAS

URE I'M GLAD

I thanked him lots for helping me
To fool the wicked stranger.
He wrote back, "It's my pleasure, gal.
I'm glad you're out of danger."

Rooty—toot—toot
And rooty—kazootie,
This concludes the story
of the sleepless Beauty.

Wait Beauty. I have a question
Before you go away.
What happened with the rock star?

Oh, we met one day.

And then what happened?

Guess!

YOU BOTH LIVED HAPPILY EVER AFTER?

Yes.